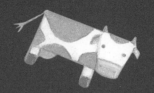

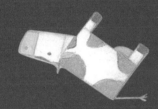

RODEO RED

To Tim, Caleb, and Rosemary.
You're the butter on my biscuits!
—*M. P.*

For John Wayne and John Graham
—two men with True Grit.

—*M. I.*

Published by
PEACHTREE PUBLISHERS
1700 Chattahoochee Avenue
Atlanta, Georgia 30318-2112
www.peachtree-online.com

Text © 2015 by Maripat Perkins
Illustrations © 2015 by Molly Schaar Idle

Book design by Molly Schaar Idle and Loraine M. Joyner

Illustrations created in Prismacolor pencil on paper. Title typeset in Nashville by Matthew Austin Petty; text typeset in International Typeface Corporation's Leawood by Leslie Usherwood.

Printed in November 2014 in China.
10 9 8 7 6 5 4 3 2 1
First Edition

Library of Congress Cataloging-in-Publication Data

Perkins, Maripat.
  Rodeo Red / by Maripat Perkins ; illustrated by Molly Idle.
    pages cm
ISBN 978-1-56145-816-5
  Summary: Rodeo Red and her hound dog, Rusty, are happy as can be until Sideswiping Slim comes to town and starts stirring up trouble for them, but when Slim steals Rusty, Red will do anything to get him back—even give up the birthday gift her Aunt Sal, a city slicker, sent.
  [1. Cowgirls—Fiction. 2. Cowboys—Fiction. 3. Conduct of life—Fiction. 4. Pets—Fiction.] I. Idle, Molly Schaar, illustrator. II. Title.
  PZ7.P4314Rod 2015
  [Fic]—dc23
                                    2014006499

RODEO RED

WRITTEN BY MARIPAT PERKINS
ILLUSTRATED BY MOLLY IDLE

Ω
PEACHTREE
ATLANTA

I go by the name of Rodeo Red.
My best friend in all the world is my hound dog, Rusty.

Rusty and me had always been happier
than two buttons on a new shirt...

...until Sideswiping Slim showed up.

The first time our eyes met, I knew Slim was trouble.
He looked as slippery as a snake's belly in a mudslide.

I thought for sure anybody who hollered that much would
be hauled to the edge of town and told to skedaddle.

But the Sheriff and her Deputy seemed smitten.

Slim laid low for a while,

but gradually he started moving into my territory.

I'd come home to find my belongings all in a tumble, my spurs missing, or grape jelly smeared on my favorite hat.

I tried reasoning with Slim. I showed him the border between his camp and mine.

But that scallywag talked nothing but gibberish. He just moseyed back into my ranch like he owned the place.

Finally I threw in the sponge. I didn't want nothing more to do with that cantankerous lemon custard.

Then one day Rusty weren't nowhere to be found. I looked everywhere for him.

I knew right then that Slim was up to his sideswiping ways.

It was time for us to go
toe to toe, eyeball to eyeball.

Late that night I snuck into Slim's camp.
There he was, sawing logs, poor Rusty
in his clutches.

I eased up and tried to slip Rusty out real
gentle-like, but Slim was squeezing that dog tighter
than a greenhorn riding a bucking bronco.

I tugged and pulled, but it weren't no use.

"Dadburnit, Slim!" I hollered. "Give me back my dog!"

Well, that woke him up. He set to squawling like
a fire truck heading to a wiener roast gone bad.

In two shakes, the Deputy was in there telling me to git. Wouldn't you know Slim would have the law on his side?

I went back to my ranch, feeling lower than a prairie dog's basement.

I just had to get Rusty back.

The next day I snuck back into Slim's camp.

I swung my rope and caught Rusty round the middle.

But Slim lit into a fit loud enough to cause a stampede.

The Sheriff showed up and well...
What followed weren't pretty.

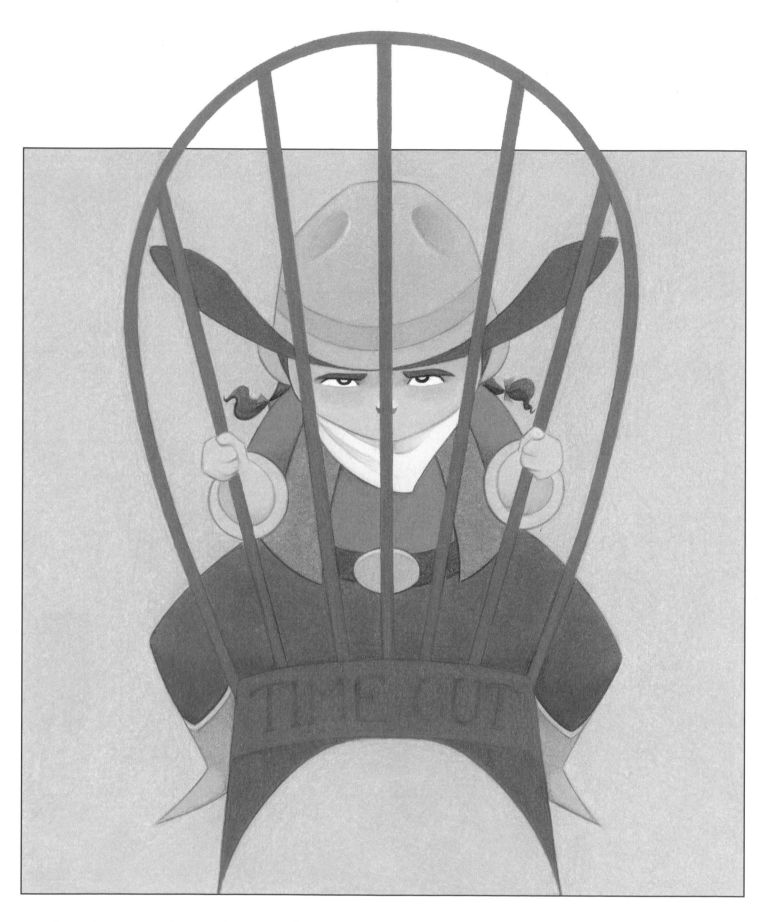

She dropped me into a holding cell quicker than you could say lickety-split. I was madder than a bee in a Sunday bonnet.

When the Sheriff finally let me out, I decided
to drown my sorrows and grab some grub.

Halfway through my second cookie, I heard a commotion.
The stagecoach had arrived with the mail.

Glory be, there was a package for me! It was a belated birthday gift from Aunt Sal.

Now Aunt Sal is a good ole gal, but truth be told, she's a city slicker.

I was hoping for a sturdy set of boots or a good piece of rope. Instead I got some sort of varnished varmint. It looked lazy and addle-brained to me. I doubted it could even keep mice out of the barn.

And then an idea lit up my noggin.

I sauntered into Slim's camp, bold as a new nickel. I had that sissified simpleton in my arms, cuddling it like it was the best thing I could ever think to do.

Slim's eyes shone like two full moons. He stretched out his hands and said, "Gimme gimme gimme!"

I took my time, petting it real slow-like.

"You want this critter?" I looked him square
in the eye. "You gotta give me back my dog."

Slim hesitated. His eyes darted back and forth
between Rusty and that fussy feline.

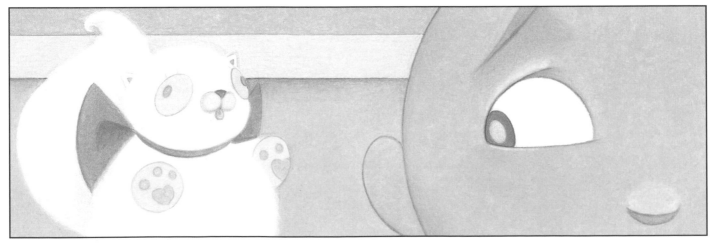

I could tell he was weighing things out.

But the sight of that dolled-up dandy was finally too much for him. He handed over Rusty like he was a hot coal at a barbeque.

After that, Slim didn't pay Rusty no never mind. He hugged that frilly varmint like he'd found his best friend for life.

Well, there's no accounting for taste, but what did I care? I had Rusty back where he belonged, safe in my arms.

It was time to put my boots up for a spell
before the next adventure. I tucked Rusty close
and we headed back to the ranch, happier
than two freckles on a sunny cheek.

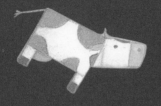

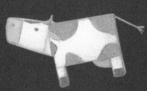